MW01047250

DILLY AND
THE HORROR MOVIE

TONY BRADMAN
DILLY
AND
THE HORROR MOVIE
Illustrated by Susan Hellard

Viking Kestrel

VIKING KESTREL
Published by the Penguin Group
Viking Penguin Inc., 40 West 23rd Street, New York, New York 10010, U.S.A.
Penguin Books Ltd, 27 Wrights Lane, London W8 5TZ, England
Penguin Books Australia Ltd, Ringwood, Victoria, Australia
Penguin Books Canada Ltd, 2801 John Street, Markham, Ontario, Canada L3R 1B4
Penguin Books (N.Z.) Ltd, 182–190 Wairau Road, Auckland 10, New Zealand
Penguin Books Ltd, Registered Offices: Harmondsworth, Middlesex, England

First published in Great Britain as *Dilly and the Horror Film* by Piccadilly Press, 1987
First American edition published in 1989
1 3 5 7 9 10 8 6 4 2
Text copyright © Tony Bradman, 1987
Illustrations copyright © Susan Hellard, 1987
All rights reserved

Library of Congress Cataloging in Publication Data
Bradman, Tony.   [Dilly and the horror film]
Dilly and the horror movie/by Tony Bradman; illustrated by Susan Hellard.   p.   cm.
Originally published under title: Dilly and the horror film.
Summary: A mischievous young dinosaur goes to nursery school for
the first time, gets a scare from a horror movie, and has other adventures.
ISBN 0-670-82351-1   [1. Dinosaurs—Fiction.   2. Humorous stories.]
I. Hellard, Susan, ill.   II. Title.
PZ7.B7275Dg 1989   [Fic]—dc19   88-28758   CIP
Printed in the United States of America by Book Press, Brattleboro, Vermont

CONTENTS

DILLY
AND
THE HORROR MOVIE

1. DILLY GOES TO SCHOOL

The trouble with my little brother Dilly is that he can never make up his mind. One minute he wants something, and the next minute he doesn't want it at all.

The other morning, for example, he was being such a pest at breakfast. He said he wanted fern flakes, but as soon as Father put them in front of him, he changed his mind and said he wanted toasted swamp worms instead.

"Well, I'm sorry, Dilly," said Father, "but I'm not throwing away a whole bowl full of perfectly good fern flakes just to suit you. Eat up now, and let's have no more nonsense."

Dilly looked very cross and sulky. "I'm not going to eat my fern flakes," he said. "They're *yucky*."

"I do hope you're not going to be naughty this morning, Dilly," Father sighed. "We haven't got time for all that . . . or have you forgotten that it's a special day today?"

I could see that Dilly hadn't forgotten. For weeks and weeks he's been saying that he wants to go

to school like me, and he had been
so excited when Mother and Father
said that they'd arranged for him to
go to nursery school.

They had also said that Dilly
could visit his nursery school one
day, before he started going there
for real, to meet his teacher, Mrs.
Dactyl, and to see what it was like.

Now that day had come.

"And do you remember what I
said, Dilly?" Father gave Dilly a
stern look. "Only *good* little
dinosaurs go to nursery school.
Do you promise you'll try your
hardest to be good from now on?"

"I promise, Father," said Dilly. He
gave Father one of his biggest
I'm-going-to-be-a-good-little-dinosaur
smiles. Father didn't look as if he
believed him. I certainly didn't.

But Dilly *was* good, and he did stop being a pest. He ate up all his fern flakes without any fuss at all, went upstairs to clean his teeth without being told to, and was ready to go to nursery school before Father had even finished his breakfast.

"Come on, Father," he said. "Why are you being so slow?"

Father looked a little mad when he heard Dilly say that, and for a moment I thought he was going to tell him off. But he didn't. He just sighed instead, and started drinking his coffee more quickly.

It wasn't too long before Father and Dilly set off for nursery school. Mother and I waved to them from the window as they walked down the street. I could see that Dilly was very excited, and he was pulling

Father along as fast as he could go.

Usually when Dilly does something that he enjoys you can't stop him telling you about it over and over again, however hard you try.

But when I got home from school, Dilly didn't want to talk. He was being quite well behaved too, so we all began to think that there must be something wrong.

Father tried to get him to talk about it at dinner that night.

"It was good, wasn't it Dilly, at nursery school?" he said. Dilly just looked down at his bowl of marsh greens and said . . . nothing.

"What did you like best?" asked Mother. "Father tells me you spent a lot of time on the jungle gym, and inside the playhouse with Dixie."

Dilly still said . . . nothing.

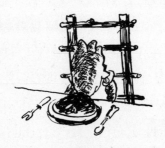

"That's right," said Father. "In fact, he was having such a good time in the playhouse that Mrs. Dactyl practically had to chase him out of it at story time, didn't she, Dilly?"

But Dilly still said . . . nothing, although he did look up when Father mentioned Mrs. Dactyl's name.

"Anyway, Dilly, Mrs. Dactyl told me you can start next week," said Father with a smile. "So now you've got something to look forward to."

From the look on Dilly's face I could tell that *he* didn't think so.

Dilly was quiet for the rest of the evening, and after they put him to bed, Mother and Father talked about him for a while. Mother said she thought he might just be very tired after all the excitement, and Father said he thought that Dilly might be a little nervous about nursery school.

They also wondered whether

something might have upset him, and they asked me to be especially nice to Dilly for a while. I said I would be.

Dilly wasn't quiet for long, though. Over the next few days, he started being as naughty as he could, and as you know that's pretty naughty indeed. He wouldn't eat any food, he wouldn't clean his teeth or wash, he wouldn't go to bed and he wouldn't get up . . . he wouldn't do anything at all.

"Dilly Dinosaur," said Father one morning, "why are you being so naughty? I'm afraid you won't be able to go to nursery school if you keep up this sort of behavior."

"Good!" shouted Dilly. "I don't want to go to stupid old nursery school. It's *yucky,* and I hate it, and I hate that horrible old Mrs. Dactyl!"

"Well, Dilly," said Father. "You've certainly changed your tune. It wasn't so long ago that you were begging us to send you to school. We've gone to a lot of trouble to arrange it for you, too."

"I don't care," said Dilly. He swished his tail around and stamped his foot. "I don't want to go to school."

I could see that Father was beginning to look a little angry.

"Well, Dilly," he said, "I'm afraid you're going to have to."

Dilly didn't say anything. He just opened his mouth and . . . let rip with an ultra-special, 150-mile-per-hour super-scream, the sort that makes Mother dive into a cupboard, me hide under the table, and Father put his head in a bucket until Dilly quiets down.

Dilly was sent straight to his room, and after everyone had calmed down, Father had a long talk with him. In the end Dilly admitted that he *was* worried about something at nursery school. He said that he'd been as naughty as he could be on purpose so that they wouldn't send him back to school.

"What's upset you so much, Dilly?" asked Father.

"It was when Mrs Dactyl told me to come out of the playhouse," he said at last. "She told me that if I didn't hurry up she'd . . . she'd chop me up for firewood, and I didn't want her to." And then he burst into tears.

"Oh, Dilly," said Mother as she gave him a hug. "She was only joking, I'm sure. You aren't frightened of Mrs. Dactyl, are you?"

"She has a big beak," said Dilly. "And very big teeth."

"Well, Dilly," said Father, "we'd better have a word with Mrs. Dactyl next week, and get her to promise not to chop you up for firewood. Is that OK?"

Dilly didn't look very sure. But it turned out all right in the end. Mrs. Dactyl said she was sorry for upsetting Dilly, and that she *had* only been joking.

After that, Dilly really began to enjoy nursery school. On Friday, at the end of his first week, Mrs. Dactyl told Father that Dilly was a very good little dinosaur, although she did say that he could be a little noisy sometimes.

In fact, Dilly loved school so much that he even wanted to go there on Saturday. Father had to explain that no one went to school on the weekend, because they all needed a rest after working so hard during the week.

"Does Mrs. Dactyl need to have a rest too, Father?" said Dilly.

"I'm sure she does, Dilly," Father laughed. "Especially after last week!"

2. DILLY AND THE BABY
   DINOSAUR

The other day, Mother said she was
going to clear out an old trunk. She
thought some of the clothes Dilly
and I used to wear when we were
baby dinosaurs might be in it, and
she wanted to see if there was
anything she could give to Aunt
Dimpla for baby Deevoo.

   Aunt Dimpla is Mother's younger
sister, and she's really nice. Her
baby, Deevoo, is our cousin. He's

still very small, because he only hatched out of his egg a little while ago.

Mother said we could help her, but only if we were good and didn't argue. She found the baby clothes, too.

"You don't remember being little, do you, Dilly?" she said. "It doesn't seem possible now, but you did fit into these tiny clothes once upon a time. You looked so sweet."

"I don't remember him being very sweet," I said. "He used to scream a lot."

"I did not," said Dilly.

"All right, Dorla and Dilly," said Mother. "That's enough of that. But Dorla is partly right, Dilly. You did scream a lot when you were a baby dinosaur."

Dilly was looking a little confused now.

"But you said I was sweet, Mother."

"I said you *looked* sweet, Dilly," Mother said. "But you didn't sound so sweet. That's the thing about babies. In some ways they're lovely, but in other ways they're not very lovely at all. Anyway, come along you two, it's time for lunch now."

While we were eating our lunch,

the dinophone rang. Mother answered it, and when she came back to the table, she said she had a wonderful surprise for us.

"That was your Aunt Dimpla," she said. "She's asked us to look after baby Deevoo this afternoon while she goes to the Tail Dressers to have her tail curled."

Dilly and I were very excited, and we couldn't wait for Aunt Dimpla and Deevoo to arrive. When they did, Deevoo was fast asleep in his

special basket, and he didn't even wake up when Aunt Dimpla kissed him goodbye. Mother told Dilly he wasn't to make any noise.

After a while, Dilly crept up and looked at Deevoo.

"He's very quiet," he said.

"He's asleep," said Mother.

"But I want to play with him, Mother," said Dilly with a big smile on his face. "He can ride my dino-trike if he likes."

Mother laughed.

"I'm afraid he's not quite old enough to play that sort of game, Dilly," she said.

"Well, will *you* play with me, Mother?" said Dilly. "You said you'd help me with my puzzle today."

"Of course I will, Dilly . . ." Mother started to say. But just at that moment, baby Deevoo woke up and began to cry.

"Oh, Dilly," said Mother, "we'll have to see what Deevoo wants now. Would you and Dorla like to help me with him?"

I could see that Dilly didn't think all that much of Deevoo, though.

"That's it, Dilly," said Mother. "Shake the rattle in front of Deevoo . . . you see? He thinks you're wonderful because you're playing with him."

It was true. Deevoo was smiling and gurgling and waving his little

paws around. But Dilly didn't look
so sure.

"He's not even looking at me,"
he said.

"Deevoo's looking at the rattle,
Dilly," said Mother, "because it's
colorful and makes a noise. You're
the one who's shaking it, though,
aren't you?"

But Dilly had stopped shaking
the rattle.

"I don't want to play with
Deevoo any more," he said.

"I think he's very . . . boring. All he does is sleep, or cry, or look at a stupid rattle."

Mother laughed, and she was about to say something when Deevoo started to cry again. Dilly had a real I-told-you-so look on his face.

"Oh well, Dilly," said Mother, "it

looks like you're right. Anyway, I'll help you with your puzzle when Deevoo quiets down and goes back to sleep."

But the trouble was that Deevoo didn't quiet down, and he didn't go back to sleep, either. He cried, and he cried, and he cried.

"What's wrong with him,

Mother?" asked Dilly after a while.

"What, Dilly?" said Mother. She was walking up and down, trying to rock Deevoo off to sleep, and I could see that she was beginning to get quite hot and bothered.

"Oh, he's probably feeling a little unsettled," she said. "He doesn't know us very well, after all."

"Well, can you help me with my puzzle now, Mother?" asked Dilly.

"What, Dilly? I've already told you once," said Mother, who was looking a little angry now, "that I'll help you with your puzzle when Deevoo quiets down. Please be a little patient!"

Dilly looked angry too, and he stamped his feet when he walked away from Mother—STAMP! STAMP! STAMP!

Deevoo still didn't quiet down, though. He just kept crying, and it got louder, and louder, and louder. Mother got more and more flustered, too.

Then Dilly came back. He opened the door with a—BANG!— and stamped up to Mother, STAMP! STAMP! STAMP! He stood right in front of her, and I could see that he had his I-feel-very-mean-because-you-won't-do-what-I-want-you-to look on his face.

"I *want* you to help me with my puzzle," he said, "and I want you to do it *now!*"

"Dilly Dinosaur," she shouted, so that he could hear her over Deevoo's crying, "I've told you once, and I've told you twice, I can't play with you right now!"

That did it. Dilly looked at Deevoo, then at Mother, and then . . . he let rip with a 150-mile-per-hour, ultra-special super-scream.

Mother blew her top and Dilly was sent straight to his room.

Suddenly, I realized it had gone very quiet. Deevoo had stopped crying. In fact, he had stopped crying as soon as Dilly had begun screaming. Mother and I looked at each other, and we started to laugh.

"Poor Deevoo," she said. "He was probably surprised that someone could make more noise than him! And poor Dilly . . . he's probably feeling very left out. I'd better go and see him now that Deevoo's quiet."

In fact, Deevoo went to sleep, and both Mother and I went up to see Dilly.

"You've been a real horror, Dilly," said Mother. "And I hope you're sorry now. You must realize it's very difficult to pay attention to you when I've got a crying baby to look after."

Dilly said he was sorry, and Mother said she was sorry for shouting. Dilly was very pleased when Mother told him that it was his scream which had finally stopped Deevoo from crying. Mother helped him with his puzzle, and later, when Deevoo woke up again,

Dilly and I played with him for a while. He was happier now, and Dilly had decided that he liked him after all.

When Aunt Dimpla came back from the Tail Dressers with her tail all curled, Mother told her what had happened, and she laughed too. And do you know what Dilly said to her? He said that if she ever couldn't get Deevoo to stop crying, then he would come over and scream and scream until he did.

"Well, that's very nice of you, Dilly," said Aunt Dimpla with a smile. "Very nice indeed!"

3. DILLY AND THE HORROR MOVIE

I like watching TV, don't you? My favorite program is *Dinosaur Street*. I don't watch scary programs, though. I don't like them at all.

I don't watch as much TV as Dilly, either. Mother says that he has square eyes because he watches so much TV, and he's always trying to watch more. The other morning, for instance, he wanted to turn on the TV right after breakfast.

"That's not a very good idea, Dilly," said Father. "It's a lovely day, so why don't you play outside instead?"

"I don't want to play outside," said Dilly, with a sulky look. "I want to watch the cartoons on TV."

"Now, now, Dilly," said Father. "What you *want* and what you *get* might be two very different things. What do you think you'll get if you don't say please?"

"I'll get what I want," said Dilly, who was looking even more sulky.

"Oh no you won't," said Father. I could see that Dilly had made him mad.

"Little dinosaurs who don't say please get sent to their rooms. And if they don't behave, they aren't allowed to watch TV at all, not even the *D-Team* or *Dinosaur Attack!*"

That evening, Mother and Father were going out to a party. We didn't mind, though, because that meant Grandmother was coming to babysit, and that's always fun. Grandmother usually lets us stay up a little later than we should, and she tells us really funny stories about when Father was a naughty little dinosaur.

Grandmother arrived, and Mother and Father went out soon afterwards.

"Bye," they said. "Be good, you two!"

Grandmother gave us something to eat, and then we watched TV for a while.

"You really like watching TV,

don't you, Dilly?" said
Grandmother. Dilly just nodded
without taking his eyes off the
screen.

"You must take after your father,
then," said Grandmother. "If your
grandfather and I had let him, he
would have watched TV all the time
when he was your age."

Dilly looked round at Grandmother.

"Would he really, Grandmother?"
he said.

"Oh yes," she said. She laughed,
and shook her head. "He was so
bad, your father, sometimes. I

remember once that he sneaked down very late at night just to watch TV. Grandfather and I were in bed, and we thought he was asleep . . . but we heard the noise of the TV, and came down and caught him. He got such a telling off . . . and that was the last time he ever did anything like that!"

I could see that Dilly looked very interested in what Grandmother was saying.

Grandmother told us lots more stories about Father when he was little, and then suddenly she looked up at the clock.

"I didn't realize how late it was," she said. " Come along, you two, I'd better get you into bed, or your mother and father will want to tell *me* off when they get home."

"But I want to watch more TV, Grandmother," said Dilly.

"Well, Dilly," said Grandmother, "I'm afraid you can't. It's time for you to take a bath and go to bed, and besides, there's nothing on the TV for you now. At this time of the evening it's all programs for grown-ups."

"But why can't I watch programs for grown-ups? I want to," said Dilly. Grandmother sighed.

"That's hard to explain, Dilly," she said. "But I'm sure you'd think most of them were just boring, and some of them might frighten you."

"But . . .," Dilly started to say.

"No more buts, Dilly," said Grandmother, who was beginning to look cross. "It's time for bed!"

I thought for a moment that Dilly
was going to be naughty, and argue,
but he didn't. He had a strange
look on his face, though, as if he
was planning something . . .

Grandmother took us upstairs to
get ready for bed. Dilly was very
well behaved. He didn't use too
much toothpaste, and he got into
his pajamas without any fuss at all.

Grandmother said she would
read us some stories, next. I asked if
we could have some from my

favorite book, *Fairy Tales for Young Dinosaurs.* Grandmother read two stories . . . and then she started to yawn, great big, tired yawns.

"Oh dear," she said. "I don't know why, but that last story's made me really sleepy. I think you've had enough stories now, anyway, you two. It's time you went to sleep."

Grandmother tucked us in our beds, kissed us, and went off downstairs, still yawning.

"Goodnight, Dorla and . . . *yawwwn* . . . Dilly."

"Goodnight, Grandmother," said Dilly and I. And then I snuggled down in my bed and started going to sleep. I was quite tired, so it wasn't long before I was dreaming away.

But I didn't *stay* asleep. I remember that I was having a dream about someone screaming.

The next minute I was awake, and I could hear someone screaming for real.

And then I realized what it was, or rather, *who* it was. It was Dilly, and he was letting rip with a 150-mile-per-hour, ultra-special super-scream, and it was so loud that it had woken me up, even though it was coming from downstairs. I got out of bed and went to see what was going on.

By the time I got downstairs, Dilly had stopped screaming. I could hear Grandmother talking to him.

"There, there, Dilly," she was saying, "it's all right. It's only a TV program . . . but you're such a naughty dinosaur."

I opened the door and peeped around. Grandmother was sitting on the sofa, hugging Dilly, who was crying. Grandmother saw me and called me in.

"Quick, Dorla," she said. "Turn

off the TV."

Grandmother didn't have to ask me to do that twice. I could see that there was a really scary program on, a movie that was meant only for grown-up dinosaurs. There were some horrible monsters in it doing nasty things, two-legged monsters with smooth skins and hairy heads. I found out later that it was called *Invasion of the Humans*, and I hope I never see anything like it again.

Grandmother calmed Dilly down, and then got him back into bed. When she tucked me in again, she explained that she had fallen asleep in front of the TV.

"Dilly must have sneaked down," she said, "seen that I was asleep, and switched channels. I woke up after a while because the film was so noisy, and touched Dilly on the shoulder. He must have thought that I was a monster come to get him, because he screamed, and screamed, and screamed."

Grandmother gave me a kiss, and went back to see if Dilly was all right.

In the morning, at breakfast, Dilly was very quiet. It turned out that he had woken up again in the night after Mother and Father had come home. He had been having a terrible nightmare about two-legged monsters with hairy heads.

"Grandmother's told us all about last night, Dilly," said Father. "But I'm not going to punish you because I think you've learned your lesson. Do you promise you won't do it again?"

"I promise, Father," said Dilly.

And when Grandmother came to babysit again, she told us that she'd had nightmares every night for a week after the last time.

"I had nightmares too, Grandmother," said Dilly, "all about horrible monsters."

"Oh, my nightmares weren't about monsters, Dilly," she said. "They were about horrible little dinosaurs who scream and don't do what they're told. And they all looked like you."

And we all laughed—even Dilly!

4. Dilly and the Picnic

The other day at bedtime, Father
read us a story about a family of
dinosaurs who go on a picnic. It
was a good story, and the picnic
sounded like a lot of fun. They took
a big hamper of food with them
and ate it right out in the open air
near a lovely, muddy swamp.

The only problem they had in the
story was that lots of insects came
out of the swamp and tried to eat

their food. Father laughed, and said that it wasn't a real picnic unless there were at least one or two ants in the swampberry jam.

"Can we go on a picnic, Father?" Dilly asked when the story was over.

"I don't see why not," said Father, with a smile. "We haven't been on a picnic for a while."

"So can we have a picnic . . . now?" said Dilly, who looked really excited. Father laughed.

"You can't go on a picnic now, Dilly," he said. "You're in your pajamas, ready for bed. And besides, it's dark outside. You wouldn't be able to see what you were eating!"

Dilly looked very thoughtful.

"Well," he said, after a while, "can we have a picnic . . . tomorrow?"

"Ah, well, Dilly . . .," said Father, shaking his head, "I don't know about that. Your mother and I have got a lot of things to do tomorrow."

"But can't we have a picnic after you finish all the things you've got to do?" asked Dilly.

"There probably won't be enough time," said Father.

"When *can* we have a picnic, then?" said Dilly.

Father sighed.

"I don't know, Dilly," he said. "Your mother and I are very busy at the moment . . ."

"Well, I want to go on a picnic," said Dilly. "And I don't think it's fair that we can't. You and Mother are always too busy to do nice things."

Dilly was looking quite sulky now.

But he did have a point.

Mother and Father didn't seem to have any time to have fun with us any more. They were always saying that they were busy. And the more they did, the more they seemed to have to do, and the less time they had for us.

"Never you mind all that now, Dilly," Father said. "It's time you were asleep."

But once Dilly gets an idea into his head, he just won't let it go. The next morning, he started talking about picnics as soon as he woke up.

"Can we go on a picnic today, Father?" he said at breakfast in between slurps of his favorite pineapple juice. "I promise I'll be good if we do." He smiled his biggest I'll-be-so-good smile.

Father sighed, and looked up at the ceiling.

"Don't let's start that again, Dilly," he said. "I thought we went through it all last night. We *can't* go on a picnic today. I have to go shopping, and Mother's going to try to fix your bedroom door, the one that's broken because you're always slamming it when you're in a bad mood."

The smile on Dilly's face disappeared.

"But I want to go on a picnic!" he shouted, and banged down his cup on the table. Pineapple juice went everywhere.

"Dilly!" said Father, wiping pineapple juice from his snout.

"Now look at what you've done.
You'd better say you're sorry pretty
quickly!"

But I could see that Dilly had his
most stubborn look on his face.

"I won't say I'm sorry," he
shouted, and stamped his feet,
STAMP! STAMP! "I think you're
really mean, and I hate you!"

And then . . . that's right, you
guessed it. Dilly opened his mouth
and let loose with a 150-mile-
per-hour, ultra-special super-
scream, the kind that makes

Father dive under the breakfast table, Mother run into the next room, and me pull my sweater over my head until he quiets down.

Father told Dilly off and sent him to his room.

Father went out to do the shopping a little while later, and Mother went up to Dilly's room to see about fixing his door. He was still very grumpy, although he did say that he was sorry for spilling his pineapple juice.

"That's all right, Dilly," said Mother. "Now can you find something to do while I work on your door?"

"But I don't know what to do, Mother," he said.

"Well you're so set on the idea of having a picnic," said Mother, "why don't you get some toys together and *pretend* you're having a picnic indoors? Ask Dorla, she might play with you too."

"Can I use some things from the kitchen, too? I can make a picnic for all of us!" he said.

"What, Dilly?" Mother was using her screwdriver on Dilly's door. "Oh, I suppose so," she said.

Dilly asked me if I wanted to play with him, but I didn't. I wanted to stay in my room and read my library book.

It was so good that I just kept reading, and I lost all track of time. After a while, Mother looked round my door.

"Dilly's very quiet, isn't he?" she said. "I do hope he's not getting in to any mischief."

"I'll go and take a look, Mother," I said.

I went downstairs, and at first I couldn't find him anywhere. Then I heard some noise coming from the kitchen.

I opened the kitchen door and looked inside. I couldn't believe what I saw. Dilly looked up at me and smiled.

"Have you come to my picnic, Dorla?" he said. "I was just coming to get you and Mother."

He was sitting on the floor, on one of Mother's best tablecloths. All around him there were pots, pans, knives, forks, plates and cups. But that wasn't the worst of it. He had got all the food out of the cupboards and the refrigerator, too. There was pineapple juice, fern flakes, melting ice cream, marsh greens and swampberry jam everywhere.

I went and told Mother, and she came to see what Dilly had done. At first she didn't say anything, and then she started laughing.

Just then, Father came home.

Mother looked at Father . . . and Father looked at Mother, and Father started to laugh as well.

"You're very naughty, Dilly," said Father. "But it's very nice of you to have made us a picnic."

Then Father had a really good idea. "Why don't we have a real picnic instead of dinner tonight," he said. "Right here, on the kitchen floor!"

We all tidied up the mess, and soon we were all sitting down for our picnic with real food.

"Oh, and I nearly forgot," said Dilly, jumping up to run outside into the garden. We all wondered what he was up to. When he came back, he had a big grin on his face and he was holding something in his paw. He opened it . . . and there was a tiny ant.

"Well," he said, putting the ant on top of some swampberry jam on his plate, "Father did say that it couldn't be a real picnic without one or two ants in the jam."

"Dilly," said Father, "for once I've got to admit that you're right!" And we all laughed.